Hairy Maclary Scattercat

Lynley Dodd

Gareth Stevens Publishing
Milwaukee

Hairy Maclary
felt bumptious and bustly,
bossy and bouncy
and frisky and hustly.
He wanted to run.
He wanted to race.
But the MAIN thing he wanted
was something
to
chase.

Greywacke Jones
was hunting a bee.

BUT ALONG CAME HAIRY MACLARY. . .

and chased her up high
in the sycamore tree.

Butterball Brown
was washing a paw.

BUT ALONG CAME HAIRY MACLARY . . .

and bustled him under
a rickety door.

Pimpernel Pugh
was patting a ball.

BUT ALONG CAME HAIRY MACLARY . . .

and chased her away
over Pemberton's wall.

Slinky Malinki
was down in the reeds.

BUT ALONG CAME HAIRY MACLARY . . .

and hustled him into
a drum full of weeds.

Mushroom Magee
was asleep on a ledge.

BUT ALONG CAME HAIRY MACLARY . . .

and chased her away
through a hole in the hedge.

Down on the path
by an old wooden rail,
twitching a bit,
was the tip of a tail.
With a bellicose bark
and a boisterous bounce,
Hairy Maclary
was ready
to
POUNCE.

BUT AROUND CAME SCARFACE CLAW . . .

who bothered
and bustled him,
rustled and hustled him,
raced him
and chased him

ALL the way
home.

By Lynley Dodd:

GOLD STAR FIRST READERS
Hairy Maclary from Donaldson's Dairy
Hairy Maclary's Bone
Hairy Maclary Scattercat
The Apple Tree
The Smallest Turtle
Wake Up, Bear

Library of Congress Cataloging in Publication Data

Dodd, Lynley.
  Hairy Maclary, scattercat.

  (Gold star first readers)
  Summary: Feeling very frisky, a little black dog enjoys
chasing all the cats he meets until he comes across
Scarface Claw.
  [1. Dogs — Fiction. 2. Cats — Fiction. 3. Stories in
rhyme] I. Title. II. Series.
  PZ8.3.D6627Hai   1987   [E]   86-42797
  ISBN 1-55532-148-8
  ISBN 1-55532-123-2 (lib. bdg.)

North American edition first published in 1988 by
Gareth Stevens, Inc.
7317 West Green Tree Road
Milwaukee, Wisconsin 53223, USA